To misunderstood teachers
and
their misunderstood students
—PB

My Teacher Is a
MONSTER!

No, I Am Not.

Peter Brown

MACMILLAN CHILDREN'S BOOKS

Bobby had a big problem at school.
Her name was Miss Kirby.

Miss Kirby stomped.

Miss Kirby roared.

Miss Kirby was a monster.

Bobby spent his free time in the park,
trying to forget his teacher problems.

But one Saturday morning, on the way to his favourite spot, Bobby found a terrible surprise.

Bobby wanted to run!
He wanted to hide!
But he knew that would
only make things worse.

There was an awkward silence.
And then a gust of wind changed everything.

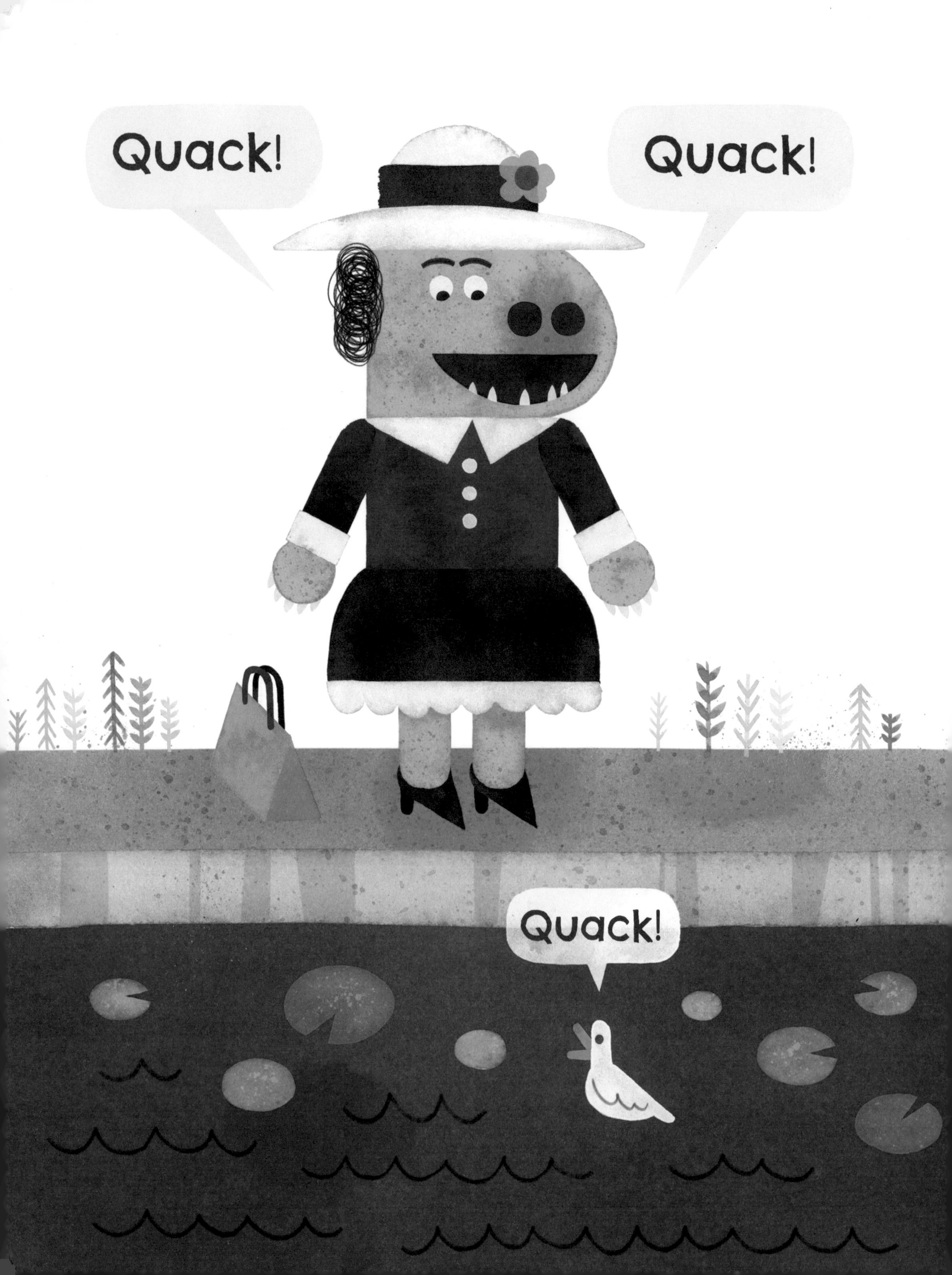
Quack!
Quack!
Quack!

When they were all quacked
out, Bobby had an idea.

You should see my
favourite spot in the park.

Bobby threw his paper aeroplane into the sky

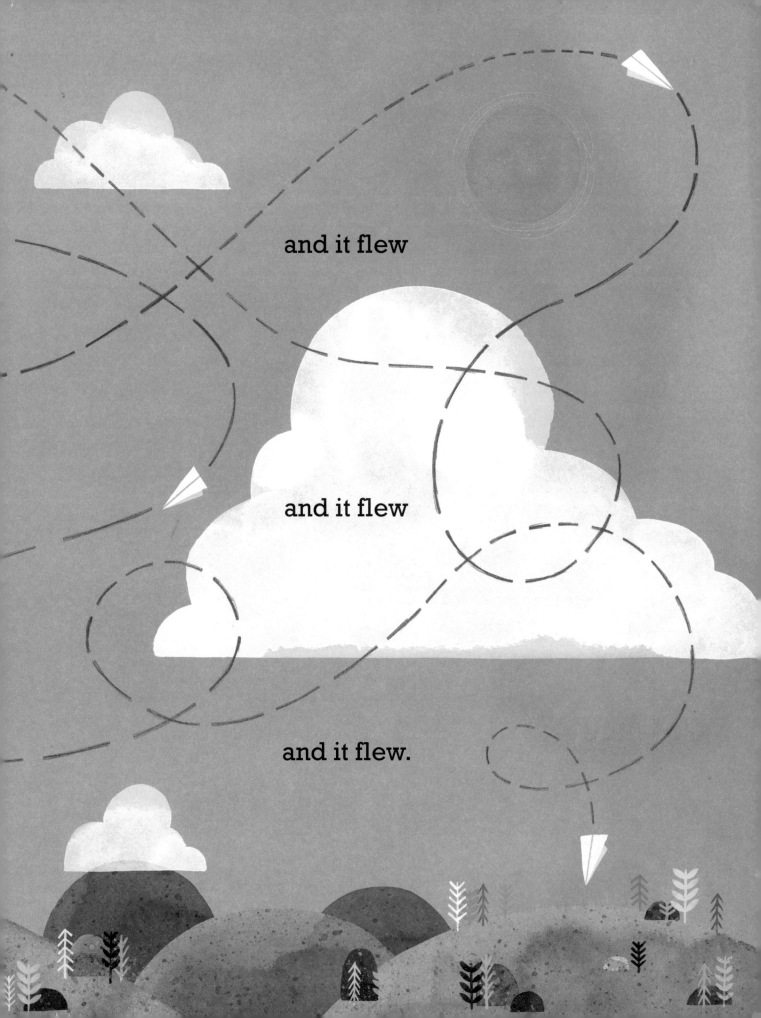

and it flew

and it flew

and it flew.

By lunchtime, Bobby and Miss Kirby were happy they had bumped into each other.

But they were ready to say goodbye.

COMING THROUGH!

Back at school, Miss Kirby still stomped.

And then the bear said,
"ROAR!"

Miss Kirby still roared.

But was Miss Kirby still a monster?

The End

About This Book

The illustrations for this book were made with India ink, watercolour, gouache, and pencil on paper, then digitally composited and coloured.

This book was edited by Alvina Ling and designed by Patti Ann Harris and Peter Brown. The production was originally supervised by Erika Schwartz, and the production editor was Barbara Bakowski.

First published in the USA 2014 by Little, Brown and Company
First published in the UK 2014 by Macmillan Children's Books
This edition published 2015 by Macmillan Children's Books
an imprint of Pan Macmillan, a division of
Macmillan Publishers Ltd
20 New Wharf Road, London N1 9RR
Associated companies throughout the world
www.panmacmillan.com

ISBN: 978-1-4472-5748-6

A CIP catalogue record for this book is available from the British Library.

Printed in China